Ahoy, mateys! Do you want to join my pirate crew? Then just say the pirate password: "Yo-ho-ho!" As part of my crew, you'll need to learn the Never Land pirate pledge.

TODAY'S PIRATE PLEDGE

Good mateys always work together as a team!

ABDOPUBLISHING.COM

Reinforced library bound edition published in 2016 by Spotlight, a division of ABDO
PO Box 398166, Minneapolis, Minnesota 55439. Spotlight produces high-quality
reinforced library bound editions for schools and libraries.
Published by agreement with Disney Enterprises, Inc.

Printed in the United States of America, North Mankato, Minnesota.
042015
092015

Disney PRESS   THIS BOOK CONTAINS
RECYCLED MATERIALS

LIBRARY OF CONGRESS CATALOGING-IN-PUBLICATION DATA

This title was previously cataloged with the following information:

Scollon, Bill.
 Jake and the Never Land pirates : Pirate campout / adapted by Bill Scollon ; illustrated by the
Character Building Studio and the Disney Storybook Art Team.
  p. cm. (World of reading ; Level 1)
Summary: Jake and his crew go camping at Doubloon Lagoon, and when Captain Hook joins
them, they see that the old pirate needs to brush up on his camping skills.
1. Pirates--Juvenile fiction. 2. Camping--Juvenile fiction. 3. Adventure stories. I. Character
Building Studio, ill. II. Disney Storybook Art Team, ill.
[E]--dc23
        2014912348

978-1-61479-362-5 (reinforced library bound edition)

Spotlight
A Division of ABDO
abdopublishing.com

PIRATE CAMPOUT

WITHDRAWN

BASED ON THE EPISODE WRITTEN BY MARK DROP

ADAPTED BY BILL SCOLLON

ILLUSTRATED BY CHARACTER BUILDING STUDIO

AND THE DISNEY STORYBOOK ART TEAM

DISNEY PRESS

New York • Los Angeles

"Rise and shine," says Skully.
"It's pirate campout day!"
Jake and his crew will camp
near Doubloon Lagoon.

The crew sets sail for Shipwreck Beach. "We're off, mateys!" calls Jake.

What is a pirate's favorite fish?

"Let's hike to Doubloon Lagoon!"
says Jake.
"A lagoon of Gold Doubloons!"
says Hook. "I must have it!"

Hook catches up to Jake.

"We want to come, too," he says.

"Join us," Jake says.

"We can camp together!"

Cubby uses his map.

He leads them to Campout Clearing.

"Way to go," says Izzy.

"We can set up our tents here."

Goldfish!

Oops! Hook gets rolled up in his tent.
"Help!" he calls.

Hook falls onto Jake's tent.
It rips apart.
"Oh, my," says Smee.
"Both tents are a mess!"

"Where will we sleep?" asks Cubby.

"I have an idea," Izzy says.

"We can make one big tent!"

Izzy finds big leaves.

Jake finds bamboo poles.

Cubby uses parts of the tents.

"It is time for a spooky story," says Jake.
"I call it 'The Monster of Doubloon Lagoon'!"

"Pirates came to Doubloon Lagoon.
They were looking for gold.

But something spooky was
in the water.
It banged into their boat!"

What are pirates
afraid of?

"What was it?" asks Bones.

"It was a monster," says Jake.

"With eight legs and eight hooks!"

"Ahhh!" the pirates scream.

Hook's crew climbs up a tree.
"Come down," says Jake.
"It is only a story!"

The daaaark!

The next day, Cubby leads the way.
Doubloon Lagoon is ahead.

"Don't turn here," says Cubby.
"That's Snail Slime Trail!"

Hook does not listen.

He slides down Snail Slime Trail.

Whoosh! Hook flies into the air!

Hook wants to be first to
Doubloon Lagoon.
He traps Jake and his crew
under a net!

Hook runs to Doubloon Lagoon.
"All that gold is mine!" he calls.

Splash!
Hook falls into the lagoon.

Jake cuts the net.

"Come on, mateys," he says.

"We have to save Hook!"

Cubby finds the lagoon.
It looks just like a Doubloon!
"Way to go, Cubby!" says Jake.

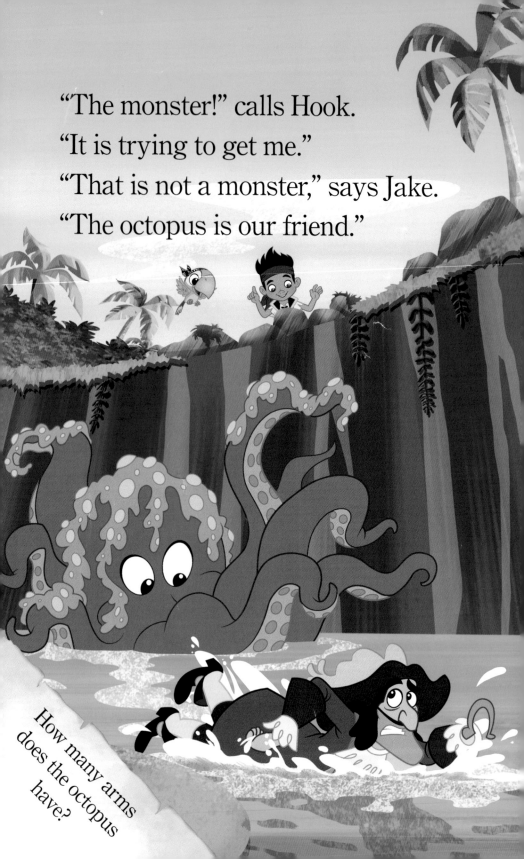

"The monster!" calls Hook.
"It is trying to get me."
"That is not a monster," says Jake.
"The octopus is our friend."

How many arms does the octopus have?

Izzy uses her Pixie Dust.
The crew pulls Hook out of the lagoon!

"Bah!" says Hook. "There is no gold here. Back to the ship, men."

"Bye-bye, sea pups," says Smee.

Can you find trees that make a "W"?

Jake and his crew camp out at home.
"I want to tell a story," Cubby says.
"'The Tale of the Spooky Coconut.'"
"Yo-ho! Way to go, Cubby!" says Jake.

31901064490909